To my precious family and friends,
with all my love and

For all who truly believe…

Edited by Jill Bailin
Special thanks to Sherilyn Gibson

Copyright © 2013 by Leann Smith.
All rights reserved.

This book, or parts thereof, may not be reproduced in any form without
permission, in writing, from Pine Tree Publishing. Please contact them
through their website www.pinetreepublishing.com.

ISBN 9780-578-12132-1

The Magic Christmas Key

Written by **Leann Smith**

Illustrated by **Kip Richmond**

Published by:
Pine Tree Publishing
Grove City, Pennsylvania

Distributed by:
Wendell August
Grove City, Pennsylvania

Andy watched the snow fall like confetti as he listened hard for the jingling bells that would announce the arrival of Papa's sleigh.

Every year the family gathered at Nana and Papa's country house to begin celebrating the Christmas holiday, and this year was no exception. However, something felt a little different to Andy. He wasn't sure what it was, but there was an extra kind of magic in the air, as if he should expect something special to happen.

It was already close to midnight on December twenty-third, and his grandfather would soon be back from the train station with Andy's aunt and cousins. Andy and his nana were still awake, though Andy's parents, his brother Wesley and Baby Ella had gone to bed a long time before. Nana pulled one of her quilts over Andy, making him feel very cozy. Rufus, the family's mop-headed dog, lay curled up at his side.

Rufus was first to hear the arrivals. Leaping off the couch, Rufus bounded to the door, barking happily. Andy jumped up as Papa opened the door, his beard caked with snow. Papa's booming voice greeted Andy so warmly that the freezing wind blowing through the open door didn't even feel cold. Following Papa in were Aunt Nellie and cousins Jasper and Cici, stomping the snow off their boots and laughing with joy to be at Nana and Papa's again.

Nana reminded the cousins about the rest of the family sleeping upstairs, and after hugs all around and mugs of hot chocolate, the weary travelers also went up to bed. Too excited to go back to sleep, and wanting to spend some time with Papa, Andy offered to help unload the sleigh.

Climbing onto the well-worn red leather seat, Andy took the reins and imagined he was dashing through the snow. The sleigh was very old and very beautiful, and was trimmed with holly leaves and evergreen branches. As his grandfather unhitched the team of horses, Andy started unloading the travel bags.

Clambering all over the sleigh, Rufus nudged each package with his nose until he discovered a red velvet pouch hidden beneath a seat. Andy took it from Rufus, opened the drawstring, and spied a silvery key that gleamed in the moonlight.

"Are you curious, Andy?" Papa asked. Papa laughed and held his hand out for Andy to give him the key – but not before Andy saw the very mysterious words engraved on it. Andy could not read all of them but he was sure the last two words said "Magic Key." Andy's eyes grew wide and he turned and looked at Papa. Ever so quickly the Key was out of sight, buried deep in Papa's pocket. Andy wanted to know more.

But Papa simply said, "All things are possible when you believe."

Andy had a hard time sleeping that night
because all he could think about was the
Magic Key. When he finally got downstairs
for breakfast, everyone was already outside
having fun in the snow.

By the time Andy had eaten and joined them
outside, Wesley, Cici and Jasper had started
to build a large snowman and Baby Ella
was showing off her snow angels. Soon the
children started a friendly snowball fight,
and everyone joined in. In spite of all the
noisy fun, Andy could not stop thinking
about the Magic Key. Was this the special
thing he'd been expecting?

The wind began to whip and the snow
was coming down in clumps. Nana called
everyone in. After removing all the dripping
snow boots, scarves, hats, mittens, jackets
and snow pants, Papa motioned for them to
sit by the warmth of the hearth.

Papa spoke in a hushed tone to his much-loved grandchildren, all gathered around him. He said, "I have an important question for all of you." Then, looking intently into each child's eyes, he said, "Who among you believes in the magic of Christmas?"

"What do you mean?" asked cousin Cici.

"He means, do we believe in Santa Claus?" said Andy's older brother Wesley, snickering under his breath. Wesley and Jasper looked at each other and rolled their eyes. Cici copied them so they wouldn't make fun of her, too.

Andy understood and spoke up boldly. "Yes, of course! If you don't believe, then Christmas doesn't come at all. I believe! Don't you, Papa?"

Papa said, "Thank you for your answer, Andy. Would you like to come with me for a little walk?" So Andy put on his coat and boots. The other children were happy to be staying inside where it was warm.

Andy and Papa walked past the barn, down the path to the covered bridge. He thought, *Now is the time to ask about the Magic Key.* Breathless with anticipation, Andy said, "Papa, would you tell me about the Magic Key?"

Papa paused. He looked at the moon, and then at Andy. "I'm glad you asked, Andy. Have you wondered how Santa visits homes that have no fireplace?" he asked.

"Or what Santa does if a fire is still burning in the fireplace?" Papa continued. "And have you ever wondered how Santa finds you here every Christmas, instead of at your own house?"

"Actually, Papa, I have wondered about all of those things," Andy said. "Do you know the answer?"

"The answer is Santa's Magic Key" Papa said. "And it is time for me to give this key to a child who truly believes, and who will take care of it."

"When I was your age, my own Papa gave it to me. And I have kept it safe for all this time."

They had arrived at the covered bridge and stopped just outside. Papa reached into his pocket and pulled out the red velvet pouch. He uncovered the silver key Andy had seen the night before. Engraved on it were the words Santa's Magic Key.

Andy was so excited that he could not speak.

Papa put it into Andy's red-mittened hand and said, "Santa's Magic Key will open the door for the bringer of gifts. This Key helps Santa find his way to you on Christmas Eve – no matter where you are."

Silently, Andy closed his hand around the Magic Key.

"Santa's Key is very special," Papa said warmly. "You are now a Keeper of the Key, and you must be sure to hold it safe with you," he said. "If it ever gets into the hands of people who don't understand what it is, who knows what may happen? You must safeguard it and use it only to ask for Santa's visit on Christmas Eve."

Andy, wide-eyed, nodded his head. "I will, Papa."

Papa said, "Thank you, Andy." Then Papa turned toward the bridge, carrying the sack over his shoulder, and looking back said, "I have something to do on the other side of the bridge. Would you like to come with me?"

A little afraid of the dark, Andy quickly said no. Going into the long, dark tunnel of the covered bridge made him nervous, even if it meant an adventure with Papa. Probably, he was more than just a little afraid of the dark.

Papa winked and said, "Someday you'll come with me." And with that he set out into the bridge tunnel.

As Andy walked home, he thought about the awesome privilege. He was a Keeper of Santa's Magic Key. He would safeguard it. Andy was happy that he was chosen to keep the Key, instead of Jasper or Wesley. They wouldn't make fun of him now, Andy thought.

But what had Papa meant about not letting other people have the Key? After all, Andy thought, what could possibly happen?

When Andy returned to the house, holding onto the Key in his pocket, he went straight to the attic room to see what Wesley and Jasper were doing. When they saw Andy, with his hand fiddling in his coat pocket, Wesley asked, "What do you have in there?"

Andy didn't say anything at first. But he wanted to show them the Key, especially because they always made fun of him. After all, what could possibly be so bad about showing them the Key?

He hesitated, but then pulled out the Magic Key and said, "This is Santa's Magic Key! We need to hang it on the front door tonight and wish for Santa to visit. Then he'll come, and it wouldn't even matter if we didn't have a chimney." Andy took a deep breath.

"C'mon, Andy. Why are you still talking about Santa Claus?" Jasper asked. Laughing at Andy, Jasper grabbed the Key and said, "Let me see it. I'm going to make a different wish. I wish Santa would bring me a red race car that goes a hundred miles an hour."

Wesley joined in the teasing, too. Snatching the Key, he said, "Oh, Santa, bring me a hundred sets of building blocks."

Wesley and Jasper started to wrestle each other. They stopped to push Andy out the door, throwing the Key after him.

Andy wasn't feeling so good. He knew he had made a big mistake.

And, uh-oh, another big mistake was about to happen. Cici had heard everything, and she knelt on the floor clutching the Key in her hand. Andy was feeling even more terrible now, and he tried to get the Key back. But Cici held the Key tight and said, "Santa, could you bring me and my doll twin ponies?"

Andy was beginning to feel really worried. He had promised to guard the Key, but he had let things get way out of hand.

Just then, Rufus scooted by and closed his mouth on the red satin ribbon tied to the Key. He scampered down the steps, the Key dangling from his mouth, with Andy running behind him.

Nearly causing a calamity, Rufus crashed into Andy's father, who was climbing a ladder so he could place the angel on the tree top. Andy's father, the ladder, and the tree almost toppled over, but his dad caught himself and the ladder, and steadied the tree. Then he wrested the Key from Rufus's mouth and said, "Even though it looks like I'll never get this tree finished, I still wish it was twenty feet tall. I hope it's the most beautiful tree we've ever had."

He laughed and tossed the Magic Key back to Andy as he climbed the ladder to put the angel in its place of honor. Rufus looked a little embarrassed and went to hide under the branches.

Before he could hide the Key in his pocket, Nana took it. "Oh my, Andy," she said, "I haven't seen this for many years." Holding Ella in one arm, she held the Key in her other hand. Nana looked at Andy's mother. "The Magic Key was how Santa came to visit when you were little, too."

His mother smiled. "I remember. We would wish for Santa to come with his bag of gifts."

As Nana moved to return the Key to Andy, Baby Ella grabbed onto it. Nana wiggled it away from her and said softly, "I ask that all in my home have their Christmas dreams come true." Andy wasn't entirely sure, but he thought he saw the Key glow in her hands.

Nana handed the Key to Andy, who had hardly stowed it safely in his pocket when Papa walked back in the door. Feeling self-conscious, Andy could not look at Papa. He went to wash his hands for dinner.

A short while later, their Christmas Eve feast was on the table. There was turkey and dressing and mashed potatoes and green beans and pie, and even Christmas cookies, some of which they were going to leave out for Santa, with a glass of milk.

But Andy felt sheepish all evening and could hardly eat. Papa told the Christmas story and Nana played the piano and everyone's voices joined together in the familiar Christmas carols. When everyone else headed up to bed, Andy stayed to let Rufus out and to help Papa lock up for the night.

The snow was deep and soft and falling faster than it had all day, and the wind was blowing ever so hard. Papa said, "It will be cold tonight. I'll keep the fire going to make sure we're all snug and warm."

"But Papa, how will Santa come down the chim—"
Andy stopped.

He felt for the Magic Key in his pocket and said, "Oh, of course. I remember." Then Andy opened the door against the howling wind to let Rufus back in, and hung the Key on the outside doorknob for Santa.

"Goodnight, Papa."

"Good night, and Merry Christmas, Andy," Papa said.

When Andy and Rufus got to the attic room, Wesley and Jasper were already sleeping. Andy fell fast asleep right away, with Rufus curled up at the foot of his bed.

The silence of the night was about to end, and the magic was about to begin.

WOOF! WOOF! WOOF! Andy awoke to Rufus's excited barking and rubbed his eyes. Could he be dreaming? Jasper was just waking up, not in his bed, but in an apple-red race car with the engine going **VROOM, VROOM, VROOM!** The car lurched forward, careened out of the house through the windows, and started circling the house just as if it was a real race track. Jasper was hollering and hanging on for dear life.

Andy jumped out of bed to go find Papa. **"OWWW!"** The uneven floor hurt him when he landed – it was entirely covered with jumbled piles of building blocks. From somewhere in the pile, he could hear Wesley moaning. Andy climbed over the blocks and dug Wesley out. Andy had to pinch himself to see if he was having a nightmare.

But no. Andy remembered things clearly. The Key. It had to be, he thought. Jasper had wished for a race car. And Wesley had wished for a room filled with building blocks. This was a disaster.

The Key. It had to be.

Oh, no!

He went into the hall and walked right into the Christmas tree, jutting up through the floor all the way to the top of the attic. Andy could not believe what he was seeing.

He walked warily around the tree into Cici and Ella's room. Cici was sitting in the corner crying. Two ponies stood by the side of her bed, their tails flicking the air. On the floor, Andy's foot squashed into the unpleasant evidence that the horses were very real indeed. **"Ewww,"** said Andy.

Then Andy remembered: Cici had wished for two ponies. "Don't worry. I'll get help!" he said. "But where's Ella?" he asked worriedly.

Cici pointed and between sobs, said, "She's in her crib, behind that pony." Andy looked, and there she was, sleeping sweetly. And incredible as it seemed, a snow angel was floating above Ella's crib. Andy knew Baby Ella would not be sleeping for long, and he would need to hurry to get help.

Bravely, he scrambled down the Christmas tree to the first floor, remembering that his father had talked about wishing the tree would be twenty feet tall. *What was happening?*

It had to be the very worst Christmas morning ever. Andy knew it was his fault for ever letting the Key out of his hands. After all, he had promised Papa.

Just then, Nana came into the living room and saw the giant tree going through the hole in the ceiling. They both heard the ponies stomping and neighing upstairs. And the red race car with its single passenger went whizzing by the window. *Vroom! Vroom!*

Andy caught a glimpse of Jasper, who almost looked like he was having fun. But the car wouldn't stop and Jasper couldn't get out until someone did something about the magic.

Nana put her hands on Andy's shoulders. "Andy, I need you to go find Papa. He'll know what to do."

Andy knew he would need the Magic Key, so he looked around and found it on the Christmas tree. He grabbed it and ran quickly out the front door.

He was sure he knew where Papa had gone. Following his tracks, Andy ran as fast as he could, until he reached the covered bridge.

Breathing hard, Andy stopped. He was still afraid of the darkness in the tunnel of the covered bridge. But he had no choice. He had to follow Papa. So he set his mind to it, and ran through the tunnel without stopping, heading for the light at the other end.

On the other side of the covered bridge, nothing was familiar. Andy saw enormous glacier fields, with majestic mountains rising behind them. He saw towering pines, taller than any he had ever seen. He saw both the setting sun and the rising moon, as big as half the sky. But he did not see Papa.

Wait! There were fresh tracks in the snow. *They have to be Papa's*, he thought. Andy followed them a long way, through the deep snow into the heart of the pine forest. He kept following them, along the ridge at the base of the glacier. The tracks led to the edge of a frozen lake, where there was a herd of reindeer – hundreds of reindeer.

There was Papa, off in the distance. He was looking up at the sky while he opened a feed sack. With the carrots and corn from his sack, Papa began to feed the reindeer, who by now had gathered around him.

Andy ran toward Papa, who was still looking at the sky. And then Andy saw what it was that Papa was watching for.

It was their family sleigh—but with reindeer pulling it. And Santa Claus holding the reins! The sleigh was about to land on the snowfield right in front of him.

Andy could not believe his eyes. He was about to see Santa face to face!

As much as Andy was excited to see the real Santa, he was worried, too, because he knew he was responsible for what had happened at Papa's house.

What am I going to do? thought Andy.

Papa had seen Andy and with his long stride, reached him quickly. Once Papa was at Andy's side, Andy tried hard not to cry, though he couldn't help shedding a tear or two.

Andy realized that as much as he wanted to avoid telling Papa what had happened, it was far more important to help his family. As he started to open his mouth to tell the story, Santa and his team drew up to where Andy and Papa stood.

Santa climbed out of their sleigh and warmly greeted Papa. "Hello, old friend," he said. Then Santa looked at Andy, and very kindly he said, "I know what happened, Andy. After all, I'm the one who delivered a race car, two ponies, and an entire room full of building blocks."

Andy slowly said, "I am very sorry. I've disappointed my grandfather and Santa Claus both in one night. And worst of all, I put my family in danger."

Santa spoke. "Andy, you have been chosen as a Keeper not because you are perfect. We are all imperfect. You have been chosen, like your Papa before you, because you believe."

Andy didn't entirely understand, nor would he for many years. But he was encouraged, and asked Santa, "Will you help my family?"

Santa said, "Of course. But first, Andy, what have you learned?"

Andy thought, and said, "I've learned that what we want is not the same as what we need. I've learned the importance of being trustworthy." Looking at Santa and the magic of the world around him, he said, "And I've learned that if you believe, all things are possible."

Saying those words, Andy felt the Key grow warm inside his coat pocket. He took it out and watched it glow.

Santa turned to Papa. "Francis, old friend," he said, "the magic in your Key is very strong."

Andy was excited. "Are there other Magic Keys, Santa?"

"Yes, Andy," Santa replied. "Over centuries I have given Keys to trusted children all over the world. When they believe in the magic of Christmas, it allows me to enter homes where there are no fireplaces."

Papa addressed Andy. "Now, about the trouble at home. Andy, did you ask for anything other than a visit from Santa when you held the Magic Key?"

Andy thought. "No, Papa, but Jasper and Wesley and Cici and even Dad all made wishes when they held the Key."

Santa and Papa looked at each other, and Santa asked, "Is there anything more, Andy?"

Then Andy remembered. "Nana! Yes, Nana asked for all of our family's Christmas dreams to come true."

"Ah, I see," Santa said. "Wishing doesn't make Christmas magic happen, Andy. It is only when you believe, and your nana has a strong belief." He turned to Papa and said, "This may explain a thing or two."

Boldly, Andy asked Santa, "I know I don't deserve it, but could you please grant me one special gift?" Santa nodded, and Papa looked intently at Andy, wondering what Andy would say.

Andy so very much wanted to keep the Magic Key. Even more than that, he wanted his family to be safe. Slowly and with regret, he said, "I ask that Papa had never given me the Key." Then he put the Magic Key in Santa's hand.

"Your request is unselfish, and your belief is very strong," Santa said.

Andy watched Santa put the Magic Key into his pouch, and realized that he would never see the Magic Key again.

And suddenly, the sun set and the moon rose, and the day became a star-filled night.

With that, Santa waved goodbye and climbed onto the largest and finest reindeer and took flight over the treetops and toward the moon, with all but two of the herd of reindeer following him.

Papa motioned for Andy to climb into the family sleigh, and covered him with one of Nana's quilts. He hitched the last two reindeer to the sleigh, and it was no more than a minute before Andy fell asleep. He didn't remember getting into his bed when they got home.

Andy woke up the next morning, with Rufus licking his face. He wondered if the amazing events of the night before had really happened, and what had become of the Magic Key.

Quickly he looked over at Jasper's bed – there was no race car and there was no Jasper. Wesley wasn't in bed either. Andy walked across the floor upstairs – there was no tree in the hall, and no ponies.

Andy dashed downstairs and found everyone around the Christmas tree. He thought, *It must be Christmas Day once again!* The entire family was waiting for him so that they could all open their stockings together. Santa had come! He had granted Andy's wish to have his family Christmas restored.

Everyone enjoyed their traditional Christmas of gift giving, family feasting, and time together.

Late that evening, Papa motioned for Andy to come closer to the tree. He pointed between the branches to the heart of the pine.

There, gleaming in the light of the fire, was Santa's Magic Key. Andy could hardly believe what he was seeing. Next to it was a brown envelope with Andy's name hand-written on the front. By the light of the fire, with his Papa by his side, Andy carefully opened the envelope to read a short letter from Santa.

All things are possible when you BELIEVE in Santa Claus

Somehow Andy knew that this was only the beginning of a much greater adventure.

Visit www.MagicChristmasKey.com for other Magic Christmas Key
products as well as great holiday activities for your child and family.

Visit www.wendellaugust.com for more information about Santa's Magic
Key and other great products in their Traditions of Christmas collection.

Visit www.PineTreePublishing.com for other works by Leann Smith.